GULLIBLE GUS

by Maxine Rose Schur • illustrated by Andrew Glass

 Clarion Books • New York

Clarion Books
215 Park Avenue South, New York, NY 10003
Text copyright © 2009 by Maxine Rose Schur
Illustrations copyright © 2009 by Andrew Glass

The illustrations were executed in oil crayon and turpenoid.
The text was set in 13-point Concorde.

Clarion Books is an imprint of Houghton Mifflin Harcourt Publishing Company.

www.clarionbooks.com

Manufactured in China

Library of Congress Cataloging-in-Publication Data

Schur, Maxine
Gullible Gus / by Maxine Rose Schur ; illustrated by Andrew Glass.
p. cm.
Summary: Tired of the teasing he gets for being the most gullible man in Texas,
Cowboy Gus goes to Fibrock to find the biggest liar there in hopes of hearing
a tall tale that is impossible for anyone—even him—to believe.
ISBN: 978-0-618-92710-4
[1. Tall tales. 2. Trust—Fiction. 3. Cowboys—Fiction. 4. Texas—Fiction.]
I. Glass, Andrew, 1949– ill. II. Title
PZ7.S3964Gul 2009
[E]–22
2008010477

WKT   10 9 8 7 6 5 4 3 2 1

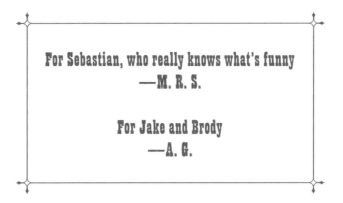

For Sebastian, who really knows what's funny
—M. R. S.

For Jake and Brody
—A. G.

❖ 1 ❖

GULLIBLE GUS LEAVES TOWN

Cowboy Gus believed everything people told him. Everything! The other cowboys at the ranch fed him the biggest lies, and he swallowed them whole.

"Watch out, Gus!" Billy Bones once hollered. "It's going to rain nails!" And before he could add "Just kidding," Gus ran to the barn and stuck a bucket on his head. Another time, Judd Mudd told Gus, "Tonight the hens will sing lullabies," and Gus slept in the chicken coop so he wouldn't miss the music.

Poor Gus! People just loved to tease and trick him. But their jokes made him sadder than dry soup. Finally, he couldn't take it anymore. He rode into town to see Doc Hickory.

After examining Gus, the doctor said gravely, "Son, I've seen some terrible cases of gullibility in my day, but you've got it bad. *Real* bad. Why, you're the most gullible person in Texas!"

"Doc Hickory, I'm a simple cowboy," said Gus. "I don't know big words like 'gullible.'"

"'Gullible' means you believe a lot of fool things," the doctor explained.

"Is there a cure for it?" Gus asked, his heart thumping with hope.

"Indeed, there is. Just go visit Fibrock. Everyone in that town is a liar."

Gus was amazed. "Why should I visit a town full of liars?" he asked.

"Because," Doc Hickory said patiently, "you need to find the very biggest liar there. Once you find him, you let that scoundrel tell you tall tales until you hear something so impossible that you can't help but say, 'I don't believe it.' When you say those four words, Gus, you'll be cured of gullibility forever."

So the very next morning, Gus saddled his horse and headed toward Fibrock. He rode through Creepy Canyon and Gopher Gulch. Then he forded Cold River and went south all the way across Daredevil Desert. At sunset on the fourth day, he came to a sign:

FIBROCK
POPULATION: 99 MILLION

Gus figured with that many people in the town, it'd be mighty hard to find the biggest liar. So he stopped at the first house he saw to ask for directions. He tied his horse to a sorghum tree and knocked on the splintery

door. He knocked seven times, in fact, and at last a voice called out, "Don't come in!"

Gus waited outside, and after a while he knocked again. Suddenly, the door was opened by an old man. He was thin and bent, like a nail that's been hammered wrong.

"Why in thunderation are you knocking on my door!" he shouted at Gus. "Why didn't you enter when I told you to?"

"Gosh!" said Gus. "I'm powerful sorry, but I thought you said, 'Don't come in.'"

"Are you calling me a liar?" the old man demanded. "I said clear as custard, 'Please come in.'"

"My mistake, sir," Gus said.

"Now that we got that straight, what's your business?" the man asked.

"Sir, I'm looking for the biggest liar in town and—"

"You're not looking for him anymore," the old man interrupted. "You're looking *at* him! Allow me to introduce myself. The name is Hokum Malarkey. I'm the biggest liar in Fibrock—and the universe, too!"

Now, most people would assume that if Mr. Hokum Malarkey was a liar, then he was probably lying about being the biggest liar. But Gus believed the man's claim, so he told him his problem. "I'm too trusting," he said. "You've got to help me!"

"How can a youngster like myself help you?" Mr. Malarkey asked, tugging his scraggly gray beard.

"You've got to tell me tall tales," begged Gus. "You've got to tell me the biggest whoppers you can. Doc Hickory said if I can doubt just one, I'll be cured for good."

Mr. Malarkey grinned, "You got yourself a deal, Gus. My wholesale-hogwash fee is five hundred dollars a tale. Payment in advance."

"Five hundred dollars! That's a noteworthy amount of money!" Gus exclaimed. "Sorry, Mr. Malarkey. I haven't got it."

"How much *do* you have?" Mr. Malarkey asked slyly.

"Thirty-five dollars, sir, and it's all the money I have in the world."

"Pay me just five, then."

"That's mighty kind of you, sir," Gus said, and he handed over the money.

Mr. Malarkey led Gus to a back office. The old man sat down at a large untidy desk and told Gus to stretch out on the settee. "Lie up, lie down, lie anyway at all," he said with a chuckle. "That's my motto."

"Yes, sir," Gus said, beginning to feel cozy.

"Now, young man, if you want me to jabber at you, what sort of tales would you like to hear?"

"I reckon I like stories about folks, sir. All kinds of folks. And, well, I like to hear about funny things, too."

"Folks and funny things, is it? Well, then, Gus, close your eyes and open your ears. I'm going to relate to you the true story of Dr. Ducknoise and how he near ruined the nice little town of Flapjack."

❖2❖

Dr. Ducknoise and His Movin' On Medicine Show

Flapjack is so small, it's not even a sneezing stop on the railway line. It's a sleepy place that never saw excitement till Dr. Ducknoise bamboozled his way through it. The first thing folks knew of Dr. Ducknoise was what they heard: a wheel-creaking, bottle-clanking ruckus. When the dust settled down to five feet high, the taller citizens saw that a horse-drawn wagon had rolled into town. On its side, in big letters, were painted the words DOCTOR DUCKNOISE AND HIS MOVIN' ON MEDICINE SHOW. Underneath, in smaller letters, was a rhyme:

> From west to east,
> For man or beast,
> Ducknoise gives most
> And charges least.

As the whole town stared, a fancy-pants man with a

top hat jumped down from the wagon and began yelling like an old-timey preacher.

"People of Flapjack, I'm Doctor Ducknoise, and I've come to fix you up good as new! You-all have a mighty nice town here, and I'm sure you want to keep it that way. But, folks, I'd be leg-pulling if I didn't allow as how you're looking tired. *Mighty* tired! You look as if you're stuck in the valley of ailing, in the slump of sickness, in the canyon of–"

"At least we're not in the hollow of hooey!" someone hollered, and the crowd broke into snorts and snickers.

"Go ahead!" Dr. Ducknoise called. "Laugh all you want . . . while you've still got the strength. But believe me, you need what I've got to offer. Why, I've made

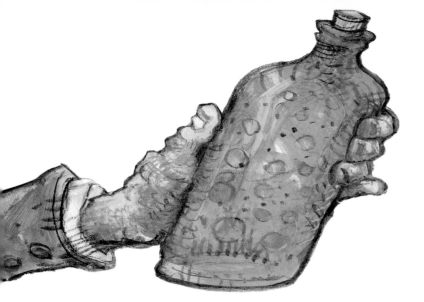

some towns so healthy, the people never die! They just keep on living till they dry up and blow away. Yessiree, jingle. There's no malady known to man nor beast that I can't cure!" Then he reared back his head and rattled off the names of his medicines:

"Calamine
Calayours
Bicarbonate of Oda
Splitspleen
Turn 'em Green
Yucky Mucky Soda
Ointment!
Oinkment!
Primadonna Pills!
Sweet Oil
Feet Soil
You're-a-Goner Bills!"

It sounded like someone calling young'uns to sup-per, only wilder and stronger.

"Folks, everything I got is guaranteed to cure you," Dr. Ducknoise went on. "So how about it? Let's start the old medicine ball rolling with my famous Cure-All Pills. You'll be so itching to buy 'em, I'll have to throw in a complimentary can of flea powder!"

"I think they'll just cure me of my money, Doc!" yelled a cowboy. The crowd laughed and hooted and started chanting, "Quack! Quack! Quack! Quack!"

Using his measuring funnel as a bullhorn, Dr. Ducknoise tried to make himself heard above the hul-labaloo. "Folks, every doctor loves patients, and be-cause you've been so patient, I'm going to let you in on my very greatest invention: Dr. Ducknoise's Smart Syrup. Every spoonful makes you smarter!"

"Quack! Quack! Quack!" the townspeople sang—until one voice suddenly cut through the racket. "How much is that Smart Syrup?"

It was the owner of the general store, Clamp-Jaw Cunning, the shrewdest man in town. He charged folks a fee for telling them the prices of the items he sold; then he charged them double if they bought some-thing. Now Clamp-Jaw stood, mean-eyed, waiting for an answer.

"Smart Syrup is only fifty cents a bottle, sir," Dr. Ducknoise replied.

"I'll take one," Clamp-Jaw said.

Well, that sobered the crowd! The very thought of Clamp-Jaw outsmarting them even more was enough to scare them all into spending. They gathered around Dr. Ducknoise.

"I'll take a bottle of Smart Syrup myself!"

"And me!"

"I want one!"

"I'll take a bottle, too!"

Dr. Ducknoise sold Smart Syrup hand over fist. Even Sifter Sol, a pinchgut gold panner who rarely parted with a penny, bought a bottle. He wrapped it in cowhide and stuck it deep in the saddlebag that his mule, Packburt, carried.

"Remember, folks, just one drop a night!" Dr. Duck-noise warned when the last bottle of Smart Syrup had been sold. Then, before anyone had time to count change, he giddyupped his horse, and he and his wagon left Flapjack as noisily as they had entered it.

Now, that would be the end of the story if human nature weren't so human. But it turned out that everyone in Flapjack suspected there was no advantage to being smart if everyone else was smart, too. Take Hiram Carysputter. Hiram figured he'd outsmart the others by taking *two* spoonfuls of syrup a night. But at the same time, his wife, Myrtle, Lord love her, was taking *three*. She reckoned it was only cautious to keep one step ahead of Hiram.

Something similar was happening all over town. Those fine Flapjack citizens outsmarted each other—and themselves in the bargain. In just three days, they'd polished off an entire year's supply of Smart Syrup!

Before you knew it, they were all smarter than teachers. Their talk grew so fancy, you needed a dictionary to figure out whether they were saying hello or goodbye.

Used to be they'd walk into the bakery and ask, "Got any doughnuts?" Now they asked, "Are you currently the purveyors of pastry with a single orifice, a diameter of approximately five inches, and a high caloric content?"

Worse even than their babble was their laziness. Within days, the town had run down like a clock that no one had bothered to rewind. There was no *doing* anymore. Just thinking. Why? Because before, the only one who thought work was beneath him was Jed, the undertaker. But now that people were so intelligent, they didn't see fit to feed hogs, sweep porches, or clean chewing gum off the stagecoach seats. Clamp-Jaw Cunning gave up storekeeping—spent his time instead making up new words for old things. Tom Jugg shut down the saloon and turned it into a lecture hall.

A year passed—but it might as well have been a day for all the work that got done. Then one afternoon, the citizens heard a queer sound—like pans rattling and washboards clacking. It was Dr. Ducknoise and his Movin' On Medicine Show coming back into town!

As he drove down the main street, Dr. Ducknoise saw that something was very wrong. People were sitting in front of stores discussing philosophy, the walkways unswept and the litter piled high as a hitching post. Right away, he figured out what had happened.

"Folks of Flapjack!" he called. "I know what ails you! Yessiree, whim-wham. You've gotten too smart for your own good. That's your trouble!"

The doctor's words were first met with the silence of people thinking. Then they started to debate with each other, using big words like "syllogism" and "cataclysmic" that probably shouldn't be said in front of children.

"You-all need a brain drain!" Dr. Ducknoise informed them. He disappeared inside his wagon, and when he came out, he was holding a large jar.

"Dr. Ducknoise's Dumb Drops!" he announced. "Guaranteed to bring relief to that full feeling in your mind. Yessiree, fiddle-faddle. Just take a few drops made from my anti-notion potion, and you'll be cured. Get your town back in working order. Go stupid with Dr. Ducknoise's Dumb Drops, the dumbest stuff on earth!"

Fortunately, the townspeople, being so smart, saw the wisdom of the doctor's prescription. Dr. Ducknoise held out his palm, and they dug in their pockets for the money.

After he had sold Dumb Drops to everyone in Flapjack, the doctor issued a warning. "My supply of Smart Syrup has run dry," he said. "So take only *one* Dumb Drop a night!" Then he slapped the reins hard, and the Movin' On Medicine Show rumbled out of town.

No sooner had he gone than the town went downhill faster than a buttered boulder. The problem was that after taking the very first Dumb Drop, people saw that *not* being clever had certain advantages. So they turned away from metaphysics to make molasses. For a while, they were busy fixing fences, cooking up beans, and planting crops. But the more Dumb Drops they took, the worse they got at counting. So instead of

taking one Dumb Drop a night, they took three or four . . . or even seven! They swallowed Dumb Drops like candy, until every single one of them was simpler than sassafras. In the end, Flapjack didn't look much different from when the townspeople were all too smart. It was a sad predicament.

Then a miracle happened.

Walking into Flapjack one morning came Sifter Sol and his mule, Packburt. He set a disapproving eye on the pitiful sight before him. "This place ain't fit for human inhabitation!" he yelled. "You chuckleheads have been dipsy-doodled by that flimflam man!"

Sifter Sol's hard words were met with open mouths and eyes as blank as egg yolks. He saw he couldn't get through to the townspeople with words, for even the simplest ones were beyond their understanding. So he reached into Packburt's saddlebag and pulled out a brown bottle: the very last bottle of Smart Syrup in the entire world.

"You've the luck of fools!" Sifter Sol crowed. "I've been panning in the hogwallows for over a year, eating nothing but sage roots and drinking nothing but spring water. Old Packburt here's been doing likewise, 'cept he's been taking a daily dose of Smart Syrup, too. Lucky for you-all, he's smart enough now and don't need no more. So you can share the rest of the stuff, and heaven help you if you don't get your brains back."

Sifter Sol doled out the last spoonfuls of Smart

Syrup, and it was cheering to see how quickly people came to their senses. They elected Packburt mayor; then they all went back to work. Luckily, they never heard from Dr. Ducknoise again.

When Mr. Malarkey finished his story, he stared at Gus a moment and then reached into his desk drawer. He drew out a mouth organ and began blowing notes, long and sugary sweet.

Gus was feeling kind of shy, not knowing if he should speak. At last he said, "Mr. Malarkey . . . er . . . that there story you told just now? That was a wonder. Yes, a wonder."

Hokum Malarkey stopped playing and leaned forward in his chair. "Don't be mush-mouthed, son. If you think I was lying, say so. I won't be sore."

Gus stared down at his boots. Then he said, "I can't help but believe it, sir. I mean, you knew the names of the people in that town. Their first names, too. No one could make those up!"

"Gus," Mr. Malarkey said quietly, "you are goose-brained gullible. Yes, you are. But I like you, so here's what I'll do. I'll tell you another story and let you pay me only twice as much as before."

"That's mighty kind of you, sir," Gus said. He pulled out ten dollars and handed it over.

Mr. Malarkey quickly stuck the bills into a tobacco

box. Then he settled back into his chair. "Listen up, Gus," he said. "I'm not too modest to tell the naked truth. So let me relate the story of Cantankerous Clem and the town he came from, Grasshopper Flats. Just don't ask me where it is. I knew once, but I plum forgot."

❖3❖

Cantankerous Clem

In Grasshopper Flats there lived a man so cantankerous, he'd argue with his own echo. Cantankerous Clem was what folks called him—I mean, those who dared to go near him. Clem could yell your ears off when he was riled, which was most every moment of the day. He'd holler if his soup was too hot, and he'd holler if his soup was too cold. If it was just right, then it was served at the wrong time of day. If it was served at the right time of day, then it was the wrong kind of soup. If it was the right kind of soup, then it was in the wrong bowl. And if by some miracle it was in the right bowl . . . well, who in tarnation had said he wanted soup anyway?

Nothing in the world pleased Clem. His wife, poor thing, put up with just about as much as a woman could, and then she left him. Took most of the furnishings and fled faster than a tumbleweed on a windy day.

At first, Clem didn't even notice. He sat in his house yelling at his wife for a full two weeks after she'd gone. But finally he sensed something was amiss, and when he realized what had happened, he got as cross as two sticks.

For days he ran around in circles, banging the walls and shouting. When he finally settled down, he began to yearn for a game of checkers. Now, Clem could bully anyone into playing checkers with him. But there was nothing around that night except a parlor chair, so he played checkers with that.

The chair lost three games in a row but never made a fuss. And when Clem threw the board across the room, as he always did when a game ended, the chair said nothing. Clem sure took a shine to that chair. Soon he was taking it everywhere. He even had a special set

of stirrups made so the chair could ride behind him on his horse, straight and tall in the saddle.

That parlor chair was a good influence on old Clem. Folks in Grasshopper Flats said he didn't bellow quite so loud when it was with him. The two of them went dancing at Finnegan's whenever Fiddle-Fingers Frank played, and Clem jigged with the chair as if it were the Courtship County Turnip Queen.

"Anyone can see that a four-legged partner is a natural for square dancing!" he growled.

Yes, Cantankerous Clem and that chair were buddies. But his happiness didn't last long, for knee-deep in March, a terrible thing happened: the bank was robbed! Someone sneaked into the Grasshopper Flats Bank at night, opened the safe, and stole every last dollar. The robbery was a puzzlement to Clem. "That thief must have cat's eyes to be able to open the safe in the dark!" he told the chair.

Clem lost all his money in that bank robbery, and it made him as furious as hot fat in a frypan. He was so mad, he mounted himself—and the chair—on his horse and rode out of Grasshopper Flats. Whether he was looking for gold or just a new place to holler, he wasn't sure. But the fact is, he was riding through the desert when suddenly a wonderful smell floated his way. It seemed to be coming from Meddlin' Mine.

"Food!" he roared. "There's grub in there, and I'm getting it!"

Now, Meddlin' Mine was carved deep into a bluff. Cantankerous Clem hitched his horse to a tree, and he and the chair went right inside. The mine was blacker than burnt toast at midnight, but Clem's stomach was rumbling like the Durango express train, so he knew he had to follow that food smell, no matter what.

Clem went deeper and deeper into the mine. "Confound it!" he howled after stubbing his toe for the tenth time. "Can't no one enlighten this place?"

No sooner had he spoken than he saw a small light flickering at some distance in front of him. Then he heard a voice say, "Sure, I'll enlighten this place—and then I'll extinguish you!"

Lucky for Clem, he was always warmed by his hot temper, or else he would have gotten the goose-skin chills. For there, right smack dab in front of him, was Diamond Tooth Dudley, the most dangerous man in the West!

Diamond Tooth Dudley stood ten feet tall—at least. His legs were like tree trunks, and his hands were as big as pitchforks. He was called Diamond Tooth because stuck in his gums was a genuine diamond, big as a biscuit. When he opened his mouth, that tooth was so bright, it acted like a searchlight. Now it lit up half the mine, and Clem could see that Diamond Tooth had been feeding on chili and cornbread. Two plump food bags sat by the dying fire, alongside enough guns for a cavalry regiment.

Diamond Tooth grinned at Clem. "Come closer so I can pound you into pancakes."

"Pound me?" Clem roared. "I'll knock you so high in the air, you'll starve coming down!"

Diamond Tooth leaned his head back and laughed like crazy. He knew he could squash Clem like a June bug anytime he wanted. So he decided to have some sport first. He lunged at Clem, but Clem was quick.

"Here, have a chair!" Clem yelled. He thrust the chair out with a lion-tamer's skill, making Diamond Tooth leap backward.

Diamond Tooth hissed and shoved his fist hard in Clem's direction.

"Coming for more, are ya?" Clem taunted, swinging the parlor chair high over his head.

He meant to do something hurtful to Diamond Tooth. But to his surprise, the chair instead knocked loose some of the timbers that held up the mine's ceiling. They crashed down around Diamond Tooth, corralling him like a bull in a pen.

When Cantankerous Clem saw this, he grabbed the food bags and ran. He spotted an old mining car, gave it a push, and he and the chair jumped inside. He was scared of shooting off into the dark mine, but as Diamond Tooth Dudley's mouth was open from hollering, the tooth light was more than enough to see by.

Once outside, Clem opened the food bags, for he was starving for grub, cooked or otherwise. Imagine his surprise when, instead of food, he found the stolen bank money! Quickly, he untied his horse and got himself and the chair settled in the saddle. Then he galloped whip and spur to Grasshopper Flats.

When the townsfolk saw the moneybags and heard Clem's tale, they were happy—very happy. The sheriff and his deputies rode lickety-split out to Meddlin' Mine, handcuffed Diamond Tooth, and carted him off to the jailhouse.

That night the people of Grasshopper Flats threw a big party for Clem and his chair. Fiddle-Fingers Frank played like a demon, and Cantankerous Clem high-stepped with his chair till daybreak. Yet all the while, he complained that the music was too fast, the floor was too crowded, and the chair was stepping on his feet. Yes, Cantankerous Clem bellyached louder than ever that night—a sure sign that he was having fun.

❄❄❄

It was now silent in the office. Outside, the crickets chirped in the still night air. At last, Mr. Malarkey asked Gus, "Well . . . what do you reckon, boy?"

Gus said nothing. For a long time he just stared at Mr. Malarkey's dentist credentials on the wall. Then two big tears rolled from his eyes.

"Heavenly hominy! You're not turning into *Gloomy* Gus now, are you, son?"

"Sorry, Mr. Malarkey," Gus croaked. "It's just that I'm feeling pretty sad about that man, Clem. Seems to me, sir, that he'd be happier if he learned to be respectful and nice. You know, I might even go to that place, Grasshopper Flats, and talk to him. Why, I'd like to—"

"That's enough!" Mr. Malarkey shouted. "You can't go there, because it don't exist! Neither does Cantankerous Clem—or his parlor chair, for that matter. Gus, my boy, you've just swallowed a perilous portion of pure poppycock!"

Gus gulped. He was so embarrassed that his face turned red as a radish.

Hokum Malarkey fiddled with one of his wedding rings, then stared at his tobacco box. Finally, he said, "The fee for my next story is double the last payment. Cash on the counter."

Gus handed Mr. Malarkey his remaining dollar bills and wiped his eyes with his kerchief.

"Don't fret, son. You're not the only peculiar person in Texas," said Mr. Malarkey. "Look at Backwards Hannah! She's more peculiar than you by far! Now, just sit back and listen up, for I'm going to tell you all about her."

❖4❖

THE TALE OF BACKWARDS HANNAH

Far out on the prairie lies a town called Sdrawkcab. Sdrawkcab is "backwards"–backwards. Everyone in Sdrawkcab does things back to front. They work, eat, and sleep backwards. It's an eye-blinking wonder!

Sdrawkcab is a terrific place. Imagine enjoying your supper dessert first thing in the morning! Imagine getting your birthday presents *before* your birthday!

Folks are friendly there, too–though it's mighty hard to talk with them. They give answers before you ask questions, and when you meet them, they say goodbye. That usually kills conversation right off.

Anyway, not too long ago, a Sdrawkcab woman named Backwards Hannah up and left town. She rode all day till she came to Corset Falls, where she went galloping down Main Street, face-tail in the saddle. The townsfolk couldn't rightly tell if she was coming or going, and at first they did more gawking than talking.

But when she stopped her horse, they made such a fuss, the mayor came out to see what was going on.

"Ma'am, I'm the mayor of this here town," he said. "What can I do for you?"

"Goodbye, mayor," Backwards Hannah said politely. She explained that she often let her horse decide how to get home, but sometimes he got it wrong. And now that she found herself in Corset Falls, she wanted to stay.

"I'd be most miserable if I could find unemployment in your town," Hannah told the mayor. "I'm strong as a feather and quick as a turtle, so I should come in real handy!"

"I'll see what I can do," the mayor said.

Well, the very next morning he made Hannah the Corset Falls mail carrier, and soon after she started the job, the town changed for the better. It seemed nicer somehow. It was a tickle just to walk down Main Street. Folks who'd never talked to each other were now jabbering together like jaybirds. Everybody seemed to have a smile to give. Even people who hadn't smiled in sixty years were grinning like possums. Why was everybody so happy? Because of Hannah! She read addresses backwards, so folks got everyone's mail but their own.

Lonely people who hadn't heard from a soul in years suddenly got mountains of letters. People who were afeared of receiving bills never got them. Best of all,

everyone now knew everyone else's business, and the gossiping was grand. Folks agreed that with Backwards Hannah as mail carrier, life was sweet. She could have kept her job forever . . . if the mayor hadn't found out about her topsy-turvy delivering.

He called her into his office. "Hannah! Hand in your mail pouch," he ordered.

"Oh, Mr. Mayor. Can't you give me another chance?" begged Hannah. "I promise to do worse."

The mayor, who was soft as squash inside, thought it over a moment. Then he said, "I'll tell you what. The schoolmarm just up and married the blacksmith, and they're off on their honeymoon. I'll let you teach school while they're gone. But mind you do a good job!"

Hannah smiled. "Never, sir! Hello, sir."

With Hannah as schoolmarm, there was a sudden interest in learning. Too bad Hannah was the one doing the learning! In the first week she was educated in note passing, desk carving, frog hiding, and ink spilling. By the middle of the second week, her pupils had given her an A in name calling and beginning disruption. She would have graduated with honors, too, if she hadn't been caught one morning playing hooky behind Sticky Stu's Sweetshop.

Again, the mayor called Hannah into his office. "Hannah," he said, "you've got more nincompoopery in you than anyone I've ever met."

Hannah stuck out her tongue the way the kids had taught her.

"All right," the mayor sighed. "I'm giving you one last chance. This town's been bothered by a lot of mean types lately. Varmints have been holding up the stagecoach and shooting up the saloon. It's gotten so bad that the sheriff ran off. So I'm giving you his job. Clean up the town—and keep an eye out for the Bad Brothers: Sneering Sam and Mean-Minded Moe."

At first, folks in Corset Falls felt skittery about having Hannah as sheriff. She didn't look like she could knock the skin off rice pudding, let alone catch the Bad Brothers. But Hannah proved to be the best sheriff the town had ever seen. Within one short week, she made Corset Falls safe again. How? Why, that scramble-brained gal rounded up troublemakers before they did a thing, stuck them in jail, and set their trial date.

"Hannah!" the deputy said. "You can't put these people in jail. They ain't done nothing yet!"

"But they're bad," Hannah said.

"Don't make no difference," he replied. "They have to *do* something bad before you can jail them."

"Well, then, I better make sure they do something bad," said Hannah.

Just that morning, Hannah had thrown the Bad Brothers in jail for yawning in public. They overheard what she said to the deputy and started making a rumpus in their cell. Sneering Sam sneered at Hannah through the bars. "Supposin' we don't *feel* like doing anything bad?" he said. "What'll you do then?"

Now, that riled her! "What kind of outlaws are you, anyhow?" she cried. "What's the point of being in the jailhouse if you're blameless as babies?"

"The lady's right, Sam," said Mean-Minded Moe. "We're getting a raw deal! C'mon!"

Hannah unlocked the cell door and swung it out wide. The Bad Brothers rushed from the jail like pigs from a pen. They were thirsting for mischief.

They got into it, too. They held up the Pony Express, stole a herd of cattle, and robbed the general store. And they jaywalked. At sundown, they galloped back to jail, opened the cell door, and locked themselves in.

"Yahoo! You done bad!" Hannah cried.

"Now we *deserve* to be in jail," Mean-Minded Moe said.

"That's right," Sneering Sam sneered. "Ain't no corn-shucking sheriff gonna lock *us* up for nothing!"

By this backwards kind of lawmaking, Hannah cleaned up Corset Falls faster than any sheriff before her. One Saturday, she threw the whole town in jail for littering. After she released everyone, she charged them with loitering. Oh, she was a terror, Backwards Hannah was, but she was fair. Too bad she left Corset Falls. I don't rightly know where she went. When you're as backwards as Hannah, it's easy to lose your way.

❖❖❖

Gullible Gus seemed to be in a daze. Mr. Malarkey looked closely at the cowboy's face, as if he were searching for something special. "Gus," he whispered at last, "do you believe this story about Backwards Hannah?"

❖ 5 ❖

THE TRUE ENDING TO THIS TALE

Gus's mind was swinging back and forth faster than a saloon door. "What, sir?" he asked.

"The story I just told," said Mr. Malarkey. "Do you believe it?"

A smile broke across Gus's face, and one little word was hatched: "Taradiddle."

"What's that you say? Speak up, my boy!"

"Taradiddle, Mr. Malarkey. That there story is nothing but taradiddle!" Gus's smile widened. "Pardon me for saying so, but it's all baloney. Claptrap! Humbug! Flapdoodle! A town of backwards people and a sheriff sticking good folks in jail? That's a tall tale for certain."

"What makes you think so, Gus?"

"Because of that jail cell door, sir." Gus chortled in amusement. "You said Hannah opened it *out*. Heck, if she was so backwards, wouldn't she have pushed it *in*? I mean, it's just cowboy logic!"

Gus was laughing now and slapping his knee in delight. "I don't believe it! I don't believe it!" he howled.

Mr. Malarkey watched him for a few amazed seconds. "Gus! You're cured." he declared. "Congratulations!"

Gus tried to talk, but he had a hard time controlling himself. As he yelped his goodbyes and his mighty gratefuls, laughs kept escaping from the corners of his mouth like naughty children sneaking out of school. At last, doubled over with merriment, he stumbled to the door. He was still giggling when he mounted his horse. He felt happier than he'd ever felt before.

"I'm cured!" he shouted. "I'm not Gullible Gus anymore. I'm just Gus . . . plain old Gus."

It was daybreak when Gus rode out of Fibrock. Before long, he was crossing the desert again, heading for home. The warm air smelled dry and spicy, and the sky sparkled like a deep lake. He sang as he rode, and every so often he laughed at his own cleverness.

Gus traveled like this for two days. Then, early on the morning of the third day, he saw someone in the distance riding toward him. Within minutes they met—or would have, if the rider hadn't been facing his horse's behind.

"Giddyup," the rider said, pulling his horse to a halt. He turned in the saddle . . . and Gus saw that *he* was a *she*. Bit by the rattlesnake of romance, he fell in love—just like that!

"Howdy, ma'am. Gus's my name," he said. Then, blushing redder than new barn paint, he asked, "Mind if I ride with you awhile?"

"Goodbye, Gus. My name is Hannah," the lady said with a smile. "I'd be sad to ride with you." She started her horse with a gentle "Whoa." Then she and Gus rode off into the sunrise together.

410

2-4

GAYLORD